Park Stories: *The Green Park*

Park Stories: The Dreams of Bethany Mellmoth

ISBN: 978-0-9558761-1-0

Series Editor: Rowan Routh

Published by The Royal Parks
www.royalparks.org.uk

Production by Strange Attractor Press
BM SAP, London, WC1N 3XX, UK
www.strangeattractor.co.uk

Cover design: Ali Hutchinson

Park Stories devised by Rowan Routh

A CIP catalogue record for this book is available from the British Library.

The Royal Parks gratefully acknowledges the financial support of Arts Council England.

Printed by Kennet Print, Devizes, UK on 100% post-consumer recycled Cyclus offset paper using vegetable-based inks.

The Dreams of Bethany Mellmoth

William Boyd

The Dreams of Bethany Mellmoth

Bethany crosses Piccadilly and enters the park, sensing the palpable chest-filling inhalation of pleasure that she always experiences as she leaves the noisy and noisome city behind and confronts the neat, contained, leafy landscape in front of her, the clipped, undulating grass and the great shifting masses of the crowded plane trees stretching all the way up to Hyde Park Corner. She walks down towards the 'bullring' trying to resist the temptation of smoking her one lunchtime cigarette immediately. Work then reward, she says to herself. Stick then carrot.

The bullring is a wide circle of tarmac at the east end of the park with a lamppost in the middle and four equidistant benches on the rim facing inward, as if marking the quadrants on a compass. She was sitting on the north-west bench with Sholto when he told her their relationship was over and that he was going travelling – to Namibia, to Laos and Alaska, he said – alone. She stands by the lamppost now, feeling the Sholto vibrations in the bullring very strongly today – sometimes they're good; sometimes they're overwhelming and make her cry. She selects the south-west bench and takes her notebook out of her bag.

When Bethany dropped out of college (media studies) and then failed to find a place at drama school (there were six annoyingly unsuccessful auditions) she decided that there was nothing for it but to become a novelist instead. She realised that she'd need a job to subsidise her novel-writing and reluctantly asked her mother to help. Bethany knows her mother can achieve almost anything she's asked – given a little time. Consequently, Bethany now works in a small narrow shop in the Royal Arcade called 'Pergamena' that sells antique pens and parchment paper. The shop's owner (who has some mysterious connection with Bethany's mother), Mrs Donnatella Brazzi, pops in from time to time and spends many hours on the phone in the tiny back office talking loudly to her family in Italy. Sometimes three days can go by without a single customer crossing the threshold. Still, Bethany reasons, she is earning money and she has plenty of time to think about her novel.

Bethany writes her novel in the park during her one-hour lunch break – weather permitting – as she finds being outdoors more inspiring and of course the memory of her and Sholto's last, anguished exchange makes the bullring one of the special places in her personal geography, a trig-point on her autobiographical map. The Green Park will resonate for her all her life, she realises, even when she's an old lady she will think of this park, the bullring's wide circle of tarmac with its central lamppost and that innocuous wooden bench in a unique, unforgettable way.

Bethany smokes her lunchtime cigarette – early, guiltily – waiting for inspiration. The day is sunny and breezy with a few chunky white clouds passing swiftly overhead. She sees that the old man is at his bench as usual, in his beret and tweed coat, his notebook open on his knee, his head cocked as if he's scenting the air itself. Hardly a day goes by without her seeing this old man. One rain-lashed Saturday, as she was hurrying to a coffee shop, splashing through puddles, she spotted him from Piccadilly, sitting in the bullring with an umbrella above his head. She opens her notebook, pausing at the title page: 'QUEEN OF A SMALL COUNTRY – a novel by Bethany Mellmoth.' She always relishes the frisson these simple words give her. It makes everything seem real, a wish fulfilled.

'Meredith Crowe' is the central character in *Queen of a Small Country*. She is approximately Bethany's age and the novel charts the minor nervous breakdown she is experiencing following her break up with her boyfriend – Mungo, Cosmo, Aldo (the name keeps changing). Aldo and Meredith separated, with acrimony and tears on both sides, in The Green Park one evening, Aldo confessing he was returning to a former love, a childhood sweetheart. In her misery Meredith haunts the park, finding it impossible to stay away and – to console herself – in her imagination she transforms the place into a small central London kingdom of which she is the benign ruler. Meredith knows every feature of her realm's few acres, knows its highways and monuments (the war memorials, the decorative fountain) its two wooden snack bars, its leafy avenues, its gentle hills and dales, its various portals (grand or merely practical) and its small well-tended copses. The park attendants, in their olive and Lincoln green livery, are her loyal retainers. She happily tolerates and licenses the safe passage of foreigners, as they wander to and fro across her territory, opening her borders at 5 a.m. and closing them firmly at midnight. She bows her head in quiet acknowledgement as the Scarab Sweepers rasp by, their revolving brushes dutifully scouring her roadways, and she wonders if, one day, her neighbour, the other Queen of a larger country, in her palace across Constitution Hill, will come and pay her a visit. Bethany is pleased with the start she has made to her novel: the scene is set – the park and its dream-life in Queen Meredith's head are well established, precisely recorded – and the context for Meredith's delusions and burgeoning emotional crisis is clear... She's just not sure what exactly is going to happen next.

The next Monday Bethany takes her seat on the Sholto bench and opens her novel. It's warm: a hot, still day. Tourists and office workers are spread out on the grass, prone and supine, sunbathing, reading, picnicking. She hears the regular flat thump of drums as the soldiers march up the Mall towards the palace for the changing of the guard. Perhaps Meredith should meet a soldier, she wonders, and take him for a lost prince... She notices that the old man is not in his usual seat but she almost immediately spots him in the grove – a circle of a dozen or so ancient plane trees planted opposite the bullring across the main thoroughfare that runs down the east side of the park. He is standing in the central clearing looking intently up at the leaves as if he's seen something trapped there. He makes a note.

'Could I trouble you for a light?'

Bethany looks up, momentarily lost in her plot. Meredith Crowe has just spotted Aldo in a group of tourists, has run up to him, slapped his face and caused shock and offence to a perfect stranger.

The old man stands there, an unlit cigarette in a stubby holder between his thin fingers. Bethany fishes in her bag and hands him a book of matches.

'May I?' he says, sitting down, lighting his cigarette and taking a theatrical puff and, as he exhales, flexing his arm, holding his cigarette holder away from him and then studying intently the way his exhaled smoke is dispersed by the slight breeze. He takes out his notebook and jots something down. He has a seamed, gaunt face and his white hair is long at the back, resting on his collar.

'I notice you're always writing,' he says and Bethany tells him about her novel.

'How extraordinary,' he says. 'I'm a novelist as well. Yves Hill.' He holds out his hand 'Y,V,E,S, – French. *Yves*.'

They shake hands – his grip is firm – and Bethany introduces herself, intrigued to meet another writer for the first time in her life.

'What novels have you written?' she asks.

'Oh, a good few,' he says. He mentions some names: '*The Parsley Tree, Oblong, A Voice, Crying, The Astonished Soul, Trembling Needle...*' He tails off. 'Almost impossible to find these days. All out of print. You'd need to go to one of the better antiquarian booksellers.' He looks at her with sympathy. 'It's a difficult trade. Very much the long haul.'

Now that she and Yves Hill have introduced themselves they often smoke a cigarette and chat for a while at the end of Bethany's lunch break. Yves Hill smokes a pungent French cigarette called a Gitane. Beneath his overcoat he wears a suit and a shirt and tie. The suits are shiny with use and sport many small, neat repairs. One day he asks her how old she thinks he is.

Bethany looks at him. 'I don't know. Sixty?'

'I'm eighty-seven,' he says with a discreetly triumphant smile.

'You don't look eighty-seven,' she says. Spontaneously, she tells him about Sholto and their break up, and why she comes to the park to write.

'Let me give you some advice,' Yves Hill says. 'I've been married four times and have had many, let's say, amorous liaisons. When a lover or a wife leaves me

I concentrate on a habit they had that I found tiresome. Sadness and self-pity is soon replaced with relief.'

Bethany thinks about Sholto and his many annoying habits. She chooses the fact that he watched television all day with the sound off and music playing as perhaps the most irritating. But then she also found the way he was constantly fiddling with his thick hair – raking it with his fingers, pushing it about to form clumps and tufts, dragging it here and there – was almost intolerable. He whistled, also: she can't abide people who whistle.

Bethany finds that this self-generated, virtual irritation with Sholto is working. Even though she hasn't seen him for weeks she realises she's increasingly annoyed with him, like a persistent itch that no amount of scratching can dispel. The unfortunate literary side-effect is that Meredith Crowe is also ceasing to pine for Aldo and, without that narrative motor, *Queen of a Small Country* is not going smoothly any more. She asks Yves Hill what she should do.

'Something totally surprising and unforeseen,' Yves Hill says, confidently, at once. 'That's what I did when I ran out of steam or ideas. Something out of the blue.' He thinks for a while. 'Queen Meredith gets run over by a Scarab Sweeper and has a leg amputated... Or a plane crashes in the park – dozens killed and mutilated.' He smiles. 'You'll find you'll be off and running again, no trouble at all.'

She considers this, somewhat sceptically, and to change the subject asks Yves Hill if he is writing a novel.

'No, no,' he says. 'It's a work of non-fiction. A little monograph, you might say. It'll be my last book but I suspect it will make my name.'

Bethany lies alone in her bed in her flat at night trying to convince herself that she's glad Sholto has gone, that she's thankful the caper and flicker of light from the permanently-on mute television is no longer visible in the gap beneath the door that leads to the sitting room. Yves Hill asked her why Sholto had decided on Namibia as his destination and she had told him that it was as a result of watching the silent images of a documentary on Namibia that Sholto had seen on television while simultaneously listening to *The Dark Side of the Moon* by Pink Floyd. 'A very *bad* lie,' Yves Hill had said, sternly. 'I'll wager he's not yet left the country.' This idea both upsets and angers Bethany: the thought that Sholto could still be in the country, still in England, pretending to be abroad... She tries to move her mind away from this topic, thinking of something surprising that could happen to Meredith Crowe, something to kick-start her novel, stalled for more than a week now on page 43.

The next day the newspapers announce a bona-fide heatwave. London swelters, London melts. In The Green Park the lunchtime tourists and sunbathers seem stupefied by the sheer weight of the heat, flattened and immobile. Bethany and Yves Hill sit on their bench smoking.

'Do you feel that?' Yves Hill asks her.

'Feel what?'

Yves Hill points to the climbing grey thread of his cigarette smoke, suddenly it judders, ripples, bends and breaks. Bethany feels her long hair stir on her bare, damp shoulders.

'How would you describe that,' he asks.

'A very faint breeze? The slightest current of air?'

'How inadequate is that? How vague? How inaccurate?' Yves Hill says, his voice reedy with frustration, and points up towards the thin cobbling of milky cloud, motionless in the washed-out blue of the sky. 'The most insignificant cloud has a proper name – cumulo-cirrus-nimbus, or some such.' He looks sharply at her. 'Why can't we do better than 'a very faint breeze'?'

'I can feel it just stirring my hair,' Bethany says.

Yves Hill takes out his notebook and jots something down.

The next time Bethany sees Yves Hill the weather has changed: cool and overcast with a nervy, blustery wind, more like autumn than summer. Bethany sits in the bullring wearing a fleece, her novel open on her knee. It is her last day at work as Donnatella Brazzi is closing 'Pergamena' for the month of August while she returns to her home in Brescia. Bethany is wondering what she will do with all the spare time on her hands.

'Ah, Bethany, hoped I'd find you here,' Yves Hill says, coming over and sitting beside her. 'Any news of that rascal, Sholto?'

'No, I'm very glad to say,' Bethany replies, firmly. 'I think I may have met someone else, in fact. He's called Kasimierz.'

'That's the spirit,' Yves Hill says. 'A good kingly name,' and he hands her a small packet wrapped in brown paper and tied with string. 'A present,' he says. 'My little monograph. My work is over, now.'

*

A NOMENCLATURE OF BREEZES AND WINDS

by YVES HILL

Odilon – dead calm

Bethany – stirs hair

Arnaud – cools sweat

Marius – grass moves

Valentin – leaves rustle

Modeste – branches shift

Honorine – grass is combed

Isidore – fallen leaves blow

Anselm – whips hair

Solange – hats blow off

Blandine – windows rattle

Prosper – thrashes branches

Hippolyte – lifts sand and dirt

Fabrice – birds fly with difficulty

Gontran – umbrellas blow out

Norbert – loss of footing

Zoltan – trees uprooted

*

Yves Hill's little monograph is bulked out with an introduction that contains a ferocious attack on the Beaufort Scale method of describing winds – 'a clumsy, primitive tool, incomprehensible to laymen, based on air-speed that must be measured with an instrument' – an analysis of his seventeen categories of breeze and wind that can all be simply and instantly evaluated by a normal human being's functioning senses and an explanation of why he has chosen – by and large – French saints' names for his notional taxonomy ('no Anglo-Saxon baggage or associations'). He has inscribed the fly-leaf with a dedication that reads: 'For Bethany – now there is no excuse for not being precise. Good luck. Spread the word. Fondly, Yves Ivan Hill'. Bethany opens it at home and is very touched – not least because she has a type of gentle breeze named after her, but also because now she knows what Yves Hill was doing all those days in the park, in all weathers, evolving his classification of the winds. She wants to write and congratulate him on his achievement, to assure him that she will describe breezes and winds from now on using his patent system – whether exhausted by an odilon, refreshed by a marius, made anxious by a norbert – and to thank him for his kind words and thoughtful advice at a difficult personal time. To her annoyance she realises she doesn't have his address.

Bethany goes back to The Green Park at lunchtime every day for a week but there is no sign of Yves Hill. The phone book and the internet provide no address and those few books of his she finds in a second-hand bookshop in Cecil Court are all published by long-defunct publishers. 'Try the Society of Authors', the bookseller suggests, so she writes to Yves Hill care of the Society and waits for his reply.

The Green Park is showing its first signs of autumn: a few yellow leaves on the plane trees, the longer grass bleached and dry. Bethany sits in the bullring hoping, willing Yves Hill to appear. Tomorrow she goes to Norfolk where she has a two-week job as an extra in a film about the poet John Milton. She is playing a serving maid in John Milton's household and the director says there may even be the possibility of a line or two. Once again, Bethany's mother has sorted her daughter's life out. The director is a friend of a friend, a meeting was arranged, he offered her this small role almost immediately. For reasons she can't really explain, Bethany very much wants to tell Yves Hill this news – to tell him that she has decided not to become a novelist, after all, and that being an actor is what she dreams about. But no sign of Yves Hill. She looks at her watch: she has to go – Kasimierz is going to meet her in a pub in Covent Garden. A bethany stirs her hair and she shivers.